MW00901153

Ace
the Adventurous

Ace
The Adventurous

Story By Silenat
Illustrated By Craig Cartwright

Xulon Press
2301 Lucien Way #415
Maitland, FL 32751
407.339.4217
www.xulonpress.com

© 2021 by Silenat Fente

Printed in the United States of America.

Paperback ISBN-13: 978-1-66280-730-5
Hardcover ISBN-13: 978-1-66280-731-2
Ebook ISBN-13: 978-1-66280-732-9

There once was a good and kind shepherd who lived on a land by the river side that was green, rich and peaceful. He had a flock of 100 sheep.

7

Ace was the youngest and happiest among the herd. He loved his home, where he lacked nothing. He would graze on the grass, drink from the river and rest under the shade of the trees.

There was enough ground for him to run and hop as he pleased, chasing butterflies by day and fireflies by night. He would wake up to the singing of birds and fall asleep to the crickets' chirping.

His curious little heart felt like it has seen everything there was to see in the village. He would often gaze upon the horizon and his adventurous soul would wonder what was beyond.

The only thing keeping him from running off
and finding out was the shepherds plea to
never go out of his sight.

One unfortunate day his curiosity got the best of him. He decided to run a little faster and go a little farther. He reached a place he had never seen before. He said to himself, "this is not so bad," and decided to look around.

After a while he got hungry, and he started to look for a nearby green pasture like the one back home. He searched and searched and searched. He got tired and thirsty from the search but didn't get any grass. He remembered the riverside where he could get water whenever he wanted. He missed it badly.

"It's better to go back home," he decided.

17

He began running home. But, soon, he realized that he was going in the wrong direction. He started walking in the opposite direction but that didn't feel right either. He got confused. The sun was setting, and Ace was finding it hard to see his way. It was getting darker and chillier.

Ace missed home terribly. His hooves started to hurt, and he couldn't walk anymore.

The wind was making scary noises as it brushed through the trees. "There may also be an animal in the woods bigger than the crickets," he thought. He despised being alone. He wished for someone, anyone familiar.

"Why did I run so far from home? if only I listened to the shepherd... maybe, if I stay put, he will come looking for me," he said to himself.

"But, will he come looking for me?" he wondered. His heart sank as he answered his own question. "Why would he come for me? He has 99 others left in the herd."

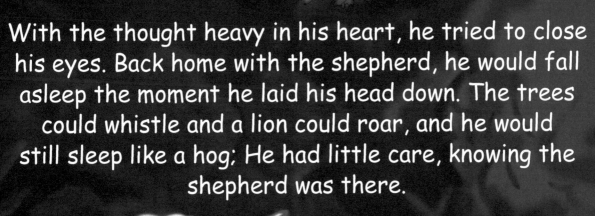

With the thought heavy in his heart, he tried to close his eyes. Back home with the shepherd, he would fall asleep the moment he laid his head down. The trees could whistle and a lion could roar, and he would still sleep like a hog; He had little care, knowing the shepherd was there.

Suddenly a familiar voice echoed through the forest. "Could it be?" he wondered. The voice came again carried by the wind, closer than before.

He would recognize that voice anywhere. Yes! It was the shepherd, calling him from afar. His ears stood and his eyes glowed.

With a lifted spirit he sprinted towards the sound of his shepherd. He couldn't believe he came looking for him.

The moment he saw his shepherd, all his troubles went away. The shepherd's face beamed bright as a day, and with great relief, he scoped Ace and put him on his shoulder.

Ace realized even though they were walking through the same scary jungle and he wasn't scared anymore. He knows his shepherd will lay down his life to protect him.

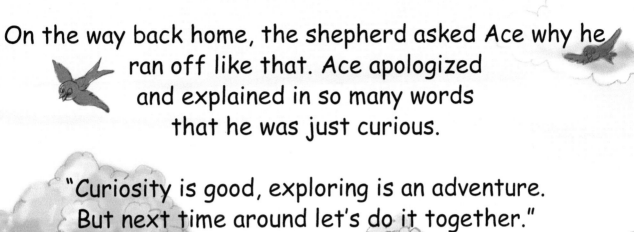

On the way back home, the shepherd asked Ace why he
ran off like that. Ace apologized
and explained in so many words
that he was just curious.

"Curiosity is good, exploring is an adventure.
But next time around let's do it together."
Said the shepherd with a loving smile on his face.

Pleased with the shepherd's reaction, Ace, the adventurous,
went about being the happiest lamb in the herd.

31

CPSIA information can be obtained
at www.ICGtesting.com
Printed in the USA
BVHW021330060421
604324BV00004BA/28